# The Centaur & The Sot

## The First Tale from the Dragonsbane Inn

By

Adam Berk

The Centaur & The Sot

The First Tale from the Dragonsbane Inn

Adam Berk



This book is a work of fiction. Names, characters, places and incidents are either a product of the author's imagination or used fictionally. Any resemblance to actual events, locals, or persons living or dead is entirely coincidental.

ISBN:1985208407
ISBN-13:978-1985208407

Cover Art by Jeff Ward

To Taliesin and Aphrodite. Please accept these humble first fruits of my labor as a token of my love and dedication. May we walk together in the light forever.

## ~ I ~

*Ten years. Ten bloody, byss-blighted years!*

Garret Stockwell clenched a wooden tankard in his scarred left hand, working an oiled cloth around it with his right. From his vantage behind the bar, the Dragonsbane Inn's common room held all the welcome and warmth of a leper colony.

Gods and demons, he was sick of this place!

The way the rough, stone walls and dim light trickling through the grimy, cross-hatched windows made the room look like a shabbily furnished cave. The way the mismatched tables, benches and chairs strewn about the reed-covered floor formed a gauntlet of back-wrenching, leg-bruising corridors for the barmaids even when they *weren't* filled with drunken dwarves, glowering ogres, and leering satyrs getting far too grabby towards closing time. The way the exotic pottery and stuffed basilisks and seraph hatchlings crammed into every high shelf and rafter created the ambiance of a musty, forgotten storeroom. Most days, the accumulated dust and bits of decaying dead animals made his sinuses ache, his eyes burn, and his nose feel as though a thistle-clad pixie were trying to fly up it.

*Why am I still here? There must be somewhere else I could find work! The Nightshade, the Painted Primrose, the Wand and Chalice. I'd make better money at any of 'em. 'Course, their service staff tends to be more of the young and beautiful variety,* he thought bitterly, as he scratched his bristly goatee with his sausage-esque fingers, and then ran his hand over his smooth, bald scalp.

Garret scanned the place as though seeking the means of his salvation. In so doing, he made the mistake of making eye contact with Stefan, the bar's most faithful regular. Stefan, already red-nosed and glassy-eyed an hour before noon, bared his brown-tinged teeth in his most affable smile, raised his glass and "tink-tinked" his finger on the rim suggestively. Swallowing his disgust, the barkeep poured the lush two fingers of his usual - a type of corn whiskey called shushang, from the Empire of Gimadra to the north - chalked another mark on Stefan's tab-slate, and turned away before the sot could engage him in another slurred narration of his "Ya-wanna-know-what's-wrong-with-the-world today…" speeches.

The sound of conversation pulled his attention. Garret turned, hoping for customers, but it was only the proprietor, Kade Wallingtok, sitting at a table with Trina, one of the younger barmaids. She was a pretty little thing: on most days filled well past the brim with bright smiles and laughter. She had such a fair complexion and delicate figure that when Garret first saw her, he thought her some noble or wealthy merchant's daughter only visiting a derelict inn on the seedy side of Angelwood Boulevard for the novelty of it. But then she'd fended off a drunken lout with a cutting remark about his sexual prowess, sauntered to the bar, locked her sparkling blue eyes confidently onto his and asked for a job. He'd known then that despite her youth Trina had potential to be a wench of the highest merit.

Problem was, the Dragonsbane Inn was *not* of the highest merit. Or any merit at all, for that matter. And, as testament to the fact, Trina now slumped in her chair as though filled with something much heavier and more uncomfortable than bright smiles and laughter. She pressed a wadded, wet cloth against a darkening red welt on the side of her face: an unwelcome gratuity forced on her, unless Garret missed his guess, by a guest sneaking out on his bill.

"You must understand my position here, Trina," said Master Wallingtok. The wiry, dark-skinned, little man sat with his elbows propped on the table, his hands steepled in front of his face. "When a guest walks, it sends a message. A beacon, you could say, into the community."

Garret watched, as Wallingtok's swarthy lips worked their way around his most insincere of smiles, making his yellow teeth flash like beacons themselves, warning all who saw them to steer clear lest they be dashed upon the callous rocks of his stinginess. His dancing Yllgoni accent seemed to give him a particularly condescending tone – or it could have been that Yllgoni merchants were so condescending as a group that their dialect had become a standard for condescending tones throughout the world. Garret had often contemplated the matter while Wallingtok railed at him for a bottle being a tenth-part lower than it should have, but had never come to a satisfactory conclusion.

"…and what will soon be happening," the proprietor continued, "is that we will be attracting the sort of people that walk out on their bills, and drink to excess, and start fights in the common room. And all the *good* people with the connections with the guilds, or the polis council will stay away because they could have their pick of any inn in Angelwood, so why would they choose one where there's violence and bad behavior, right? And all these things, they are very, very, *ve-ry*, what? That's right. *Bad -- for -- business!*"

*So's having your workers fantasizing about disemboweling you every time you give them one of your "little talks"*, thought Garret, as he grabbed another tankard and assaulted it with his polishing cloth.

"So," Master Wallingtok concluded, "the next time you see a guest doing something even a little bit suspicious, talk to our staveman, or Garret, or myself even! Because we cannot be allowing scummy people to come in and take advantage of us. It's bad for business. Very bad for business. Now, I think

I've said enough on the matter. If you are up to it, I would very much like for you to help Maggie set the tables for lunch."

"Um, sir?" said Trina in a small, quavering tone that made Garret's chest feel inexplicably hot and trembly inside. "If it's all right, I think I need to sit a while longer."

"Very well," said the proprietor as he bounced to his feet, "I have to go to my meeting now with the Vintners Guild. When I get back you will be working. Or maybe you will be gone. Out looking for a less dangerous job, yes?" He smiled as though he were making a joke rather than a veiled threat, and the barmaid shook her head, giving a wan smile and a nervous whimper of a laugh in response. With that, the innkeeper rose and stalked out the front door muttering something under his breath about "Freelandish animals" and "narrowing profit margins".

Garret waited for the door to close, then dropped his tankard (now polished to a radiant gleam), and left the bar to sit at the table with Trina. He took the seat next to her, more out of not wanting his backside occupying the same place as his wretched employer than out of any conscious desire to get close to the barmaid (although her proximity, he would reflect later that evening just before falling asleep, *was* a rather pleasant bonus), and gave her a platonic pat on the arm.

"Listen," he said, "you did fine. Nobody's blaming you for letting that shestmog walk on his bill. Not even Master Wallingtok. He just lost some money and he's taking out his frustrations on you. Like he does with all of us."

"Thought as much," Trina sighed. "Gods, if I wasn't so dizzy right now, I think I might have knocked that quince-bitten fake smile off his mog with a peppermill."

Garret laughed. Then she shifted the rag she was holding against the side of her face, and the barkeep felt his expression darken as a drop of blood trickled down her pale cheek.

"You should get a bandage on that."

"I'll go get one," she said, starting to rise. "There's a patch kit in the kitchen, right?"

"No, no, sit, sit," said Garret as he got up, bustled across the floor, and jumped behind the bar. "Kade never keeps his patch kit stocked, so I started bringing my own, years ago." He reached behind the lager cask and grabbed a small, pine box packed with tiny bottles and tins of salves and ointments, then returned to the table and presented it to Trina.

"Garret, you're amazing," she said, giving her temple a final dab with the rag and opening the box. "Honestly, I don't think I could take this place if it weren't for you."

Garret said the only thing he could imagine saying to such flattery, which was a dismissive sniff and a self-effacing, "Baah!"

"Listen," said Trina, setting the box to one side for the moment, "if your shift ends before mine, would you mind waiting around? I'm trying to save up for a deposit for my own flat, and I don't want to spend half my tips on a gary-coach. And I don't exactly feel safe walking alone right now, if you know what I mean."

Garret tried to reply, but for some reason, several dozen thoughts tried to jump out of his mouth at once. "I, ah… that would be, I guess I could – I mean, of course! Yes, of course. It's a perfectly appropriate thing to, ah, to…"

*Just "yes", you idiot! By the Abyss, how hard is it to say one bloody word?*

Trina rose to her feet and silenced the barkeep's blathering with one of her dazzling smiles as she grabbed his hand and gave it a squeeze.

"You're sweet. I'm going to go to the washroom and see if I can put myself back together now."

"You're sure you're okay?"

"Just a little woozy. Like I've had a few drinks is all. I'm sure it'll pass."

As she walked to the washroom, Garrett told himself he was watching her walk to check for any unsteadiness in her gait, not to admire the supple young curves clenching and swaying under her flower-frilled blouse and embroidered, brown skirt.

"Nice view," said a voice by his ear, making him jump.

"G'on, Maggie! You know me better than that."

Garret twisted in his seat to see Maggie smiling down at him, rosy cheeks shining, red hair spilling in a curly cascade down her back, buxom-and-then-some figure only barely restrained by her blouse and bodice. She was the inn's head barmaid and, next to him, longest-standing employee. They'd been friends since she'd started seven years back, but never any more than that. He respected her too much to try to saddle her with a bald, scarred, unskilled piece of ballast like himself.

"I know you haven't wet your wand in over a year," she said, bending as she stepped back to put her hazel eyes level with his, her enormous breasts swinging like pregnant tree-apes beneath. "So it's only a matter of time before some pretty face starts making you think with your little head instead of your big one."

Garret sniffed. "Way my life's turned out I can't say I've ever found one head to be any smarter than the other."

"You just watch yourself, Garret. The pretty ones are the most dangerous when they start to realize just what their prettiness can get them."

"Like a punch in the face?" he retorted, more hotly than he'd intended.

"Hey, beefshanks, cool off a notch! I mean no disrespect to our little flax-haired friend there. Just trying to remind you people in these parts usually aren't as innocent as they seem. This is Angelwood, remember? Where everyone has an *angle*."

Garret rolled his eyes. Gods, he hated that old cliché! The only thing more annoying than puns were almost-puns.

"And speaking of which," Maggie continued jerking a thumb behind her where a well-dressed young man had now joined Stefan at the bar. "might want to check on your new customer before our resident tippler scares him off."

Maggie gave him a wink and silently mouthed the word "Money!" while making a cupping gesture with her hand indicating a purse laden with silver marks. Garret gave her a wry smile in return, then rose and approached his new customer. He was a tall, trim broomstick of a man with fair skin and a full head of dark hair, parted in the middle so it flopped about rakishly on either side of his olive-skinned brow. He wore a black and gold brocaded doublet, a white shirt with flared sleeves and hose that was a deep and expensive shade of purple. In spite of the man's fine clothes, however, the barkeep had his misgivings. The only wealthy customers that patronized the Dragonsbane were pimps, merchants on illicit outings with their mistresses, or mid-level ruffians of the Black Zinnias, the Fearless Heroes, or some other local gang. None of these ever showed up in the light of the day, however, which meant that whoever *this* popinjay was, he was most likely selling something.

"..that was back in Medan, of course, where I was something of a legend." The man was recounting some tale from his past to Stefan, while the drunkard stared at him in a slack-jawed daze. "But I don't mind starting over from scratch. To be honest, the life of a palace bard was turning into a dreadful bore: dining on the finest wines and meats every night, accompanying noblemen on their hunts and social gatherings, bedding the fairest courtly ladies when their lords were tending to affairs of state. It just got so tedious. No, here – right here in Angelwood, Jewel of the Freelands – *this* is where life happens! Walking the streets, playing in common rooms and pavilions, never knowing who will be the patron of your next meal. That's what minstreling's really all about!"

*Great,* thought Garret, as he noticed the lute-case propped against the bar by the newcomer's finely-hosed legs. *Just what we need in here – another rot-pocked minstrel.* Ever since Angelwood had become home to The Pit – the largest, most glorious amphitheatre in all the Freelands – the polis had become home to more minstrels than the beds on the floor above had fleas and tine-worms.

Stefan, meanwhile, was following the musician's banter with all the comprehension of an eyeless mole-rat. "M'sorry," he said, "do I know you?"

"I fear not, my friend, but you may know *of* me. Perchance, you've seen me minstrel at the Blasted Anvil, or one of the many booths and apple crates surrounding The Pit on Favadays. Allow me to introduce myself: I am Farian Daringsford, minstrel, tumbler, and performer of – "

"What'n the byss kind o' poofy name's that?!"

"Ah-ha, good sir, it's actually, ah – "

"Garret! This one here says 'is name's Fairy Anne!"

"It's Farian! Far-yan. It's Old Medanite for 'well-travelled' – "

"Asked if I'd ever seen him menstruate!"

"Look, you old sot – !"

"All right, you two, that's enough," said Garret as he stepped behind the bar. "Stefan, leave the man alone and drink your whiskey. And you, sir… you going to order something, or do I have to hear your entire life's story beforehand?"

"Fair enough, fair enough," said Farian the minstrel, rising from his seat and affecting a more splendid posture. "And might I add that I heartily admire the way you are executing your duties as a barkeep. I myself have often remarked that a good barkeep must be equal parts diplomat and – "

"Ye gods! Get to the point already! What can I get you?"

"A job."

Garret barely managed to stifle his first reaction, which was to throw back his head and howl like a madman. "Uh, *beg* pardon?"

"You see, while my talents as a minstrel are beyond question, I have only been in Angelwood for just short of a year. And while my burgeoning career is full of promise, it can be somewhat lacking in the area of regular pay. So my proposal, good sir, is that you and your employer utilize my considerable talents as an orator and entertainer in a slightly more mundane capacity – "

"No."

"Ah-ha, good sir, but you haven't even heard – "

"You think you're the first minstrel that ever wanted to work part-time in a tavern to pay his rent? The Painted Primrose's barkeep's composed sonnets for over fifty varieties of liquor, for gods' sake. Difference between him and you's that he, unlike most of the poofies, dandies, and popinjays in the minstrelling racket, actually knows something about tending a bar!" Garret, felt a little light-headed then and worried that he might have overstepped the bounds of propriety with this annoying, yet still potentially paying customer. To cover his fluster, he reached for the bottle of shushang whiskey, even though he had not heard Stefan call for another. Stefan, for his part, made no objection.

If, however, Master Daringsford was at all nonplussed by Garret's surliness, he made no sign. "Now, now, good sir, I really think you should reconsider. After all, this is Angelwood. Where every business needs an *angle* -- "

*Yep, still annoying.*

" -- and I said as much to Kade Wallingtok, last time we spoke. He agreed with me."

"Oh, I've no doubt Wallingtok agreed with you," said Garret. He started to pour another two fingers of whiskey into Stefan's cup, then froze. "Wait, what do you mean '*last* time'?"

"Oh, Kade and I go way back," said the bard, and Garret felt his stomach drop into a big, roiling vat of chagrin. Before the barkeep could recover, the minstrel grabbed the neck of the shushang bottle still hovering above Stefan's glass and tossed it into the air. "You see, I knew him back in Yllgon, when he was the junior master overseer for the Bembi-Rashai shipping company." He tossed the bottle about as he spoke, making it dance and spin every which way before coming to rest precariously on his chin.

"He hired me to sing some ballads at a company party he was throwing," he continued, making the bottle hop from his chin to the top of his head without missing a beat. "And he was so impressed that he insisted I be present at nearly every function he presided over ever since. Singing, juggling, tumbling, reciting plays and poetry. Now he believes these talents in a barkeep might breathe a little more life into this place." With practiced precision, he let the bottle fall from his head in such a way that it rolled down his arm to where he caught it at just the right angle to pour Stefan's drink. "As you can see."

Garret grabbed the bottle before it could pour a drop over two fingers, and snatched it out of the minstrel's hands.

"All I can see is a damned fool coming within a hair's breadth of breaking a five-mark bottle of liquor. Now get out of my bar before I shove my ice-pick up your bung, and tell the cook we're having bard-kabobs as tonight's special!"

...is what he *wanted* to say. But of course, he could not. This was, after all, a friend of the inn's proprietor. Or so he claimed.

So instead, Garret bared his grinding teeth in a grin, feeling every sinew of his soul strain to its breaking point as he said, "Yes, that's all very impressive, and I'm sure you'd be a *wonderful* addition to our staff. Now, er, exactly how long ago was it that you first met Master Wallingtok?"

"Thirteen years."

*Damn,* thought Garret, *the story checks out. At least so far. Kade* did *work for Bembi-Rashai before he took over proprietorship here eleven years ago. Of course, Wallingtok* does *share that fact with nearly everyone he encounters.*

"Fascinating. So, if you'll just leave your contact information, I'll be sure to discuss all this with the proprietor as soon as he gets back from his meeting."

"Well, okay, if you're sure about that. Of course, Kade *did* say that if I hadn't signed an employment contract by the time he got back from his meeting with the Vintners Guild that 'we will be having very, very bad consequences indeed'."

Daringsford wagged his finger, mimicking Wallingtok's Yllgoni accent so perfectly, it made the hairs on the back of Garret's neck stand on end.

"Truth to tell," the bard continued, looking around the common room as though noticing it for the first time, "I *should* probably take that job offer at the Nightshade. *Or* the one at the Wand and Chalice. I really only stopped by as a favor to ol' Tokky. But if you're just going to give me the run around -- "

"No, no, I wouldn't don't that. It's just, I really *do* need to consult with Master Wallingtok before…"

"Sir! I have just spoken to Master Wallingtok. And he assured me in no uncertain terms that you, and you alone were in charge of hiring barkeeps because, and I quote, 'I am having far too many things to deal with that I should be bothered with telling one tipple-tossing vagrant from another'. Now if you're going to tell me that I am to be passed back and forth between the two of you like some Gimadran whore on Gim Tang Way while my landlord tosses me out on the street, then I will simply go and find employment elsewhere!"

"Right," said Garret, taking a breath and running a trembling hand over his scalp. "I suppose I'll have to get you a contract then."

Garret motioned to Maggie to watch the bar while he was gone, then stalked across the floor to Kade's office. *Can't believe I'm going to be working with this kullbung,* he fumed to himself. *Pock Kade for not taking more of an interest in his own hiring process. Pock Angelwood with all its guilds and alliances making it impossible for anyone to hire anyone without signing a year's employment contract. And pock me for not having the good sense to leave this shest-pit of a town years ago!*

Still, there was something about the minstrel's story that did not add up. As Garret crammed himself into the tiny office and shuffled through the stacks of parchments on the various stained and splintery shelves, he mulled it over in his head. Certainly Kade Wallingtok was not the greatest judge of character on Ardyn, but he never struck Garret as one to hire his friends so impulsively. Or even *have* friends for that matter! Besides, one did not live in Angelwood as long as Garret had without developing a certain sixth sense about being taken advantage of – "a nose for trollshest" as he often described it. And something about this whole situation stunk.

At last Garret found Wallingtok's stack of employment contracts. He grabbed one along with a quill, inkpot and vial of sand, and carefully made his way back to the bar, wracking his brain at every step for some way to catch Fairy Anne, the kullbung bard, in an act of deception.

"So… you knew Wallingtok back in his Bembi-Reshai days," he said as he reentered the bar, and made a show of finding a dry spot on the back counter to place the contract.

Daringsford nodded, but before he could reply, Maggie came jogging (and jiggling) breathlessly up to the bar.

"Garret! Can you take a table? I can't find Trina! Lunch rush just hit. I'm serving three parties already, and one of them wants to see the cheese platter!"

Garret shrugged and made a helpless nothing-I-can-do gesture. The barmaid glared in response and jotted drinks on the order-slate at the end of the bar in a flurry of chalk dust and curses.

"Now," said the barkeep, turning back to the minstrel, casually wiping the spot in front of him with a dry cloth, and carefully arranging contract and quill. "Why *did* the ol' boy ever leave that shipping company in the first place?"

"You know, he's never really given me a straight answer on that one."

*I'll* bet *he hasn't.* Garret clenched his teeth as he smiled and placed the contract in front of the bard, then turned to work on Maggie's drink order.

"Be sure to look that contract over carefully before you sign," he said, stalling for time as he tried to think of *something* about Kade that only he would know. "Wallingtok added a few clauses of his own that some find disagreeable."

"Did he now?" said the bard, a look of consternation marring, for a moment, his flawless veneer. "Heh, isn't that just like ol' Tokky. Playing by his own rules and all that?"

Immediately, he began looking at the contract more closely, hunching a bit as he scanned the tight-packed lines of legal jargon for undesirable phrases. Freelandish contracts were nothing to be taken lightly. The polis council in

Angelwood had each one enchanted by Lascivian Mages so that the proper authorities would be alerted as soon as an employer or employee violated any of their clauses. Penalties for contract violation in the Freelands ranged from hefty fines, to indentured servitude, and even time in prison.

"So what part of Yllgon was it where you and Kade first met?" asked Garret as he poured three lagers and two red wines, then put them on the service bar.

"Bobaport," said Farian without missing a beat. "Beautiful town. Mild weather most of the year, not like the rest of the Yllgoni coast."

"Funny," said Garret, fighting the urge to chuckle as he turned to a block of ice in a shallow pan on the back counter and began chipping chunks into a whiskey glass with his pick, "I'd heard Kade worked in Salla Bay. That's about three days travel to the north of Bobaport, isn't it?"

"Four, actually. Bembi-Reshai sent him down the coast on business. Something about going over a damage report on a shipwreck. *Selena's Pearl*, I think it was. Anyway, the company put him up at an inn called Hawespiper's Haven, at which I happened to be performing."

*Still makes sense, blast it,* thought Garret as he poured the whiskey on the rocks, set it next to the wines and lagers, and checked the service slate. *The business trip, the inn.* Selena's Pearl *even sounds like the proper name of an Yllgoni ship. Smarmy little pockstocker knows his business.*

"Garret!" Maggie's distressed voice broke his reverie. "A goblin family with six younglings just walked in, one of my parties needs to get to a business meeting, and Trina won't come out of the washroom! Could you *please* take one of my tables?"

"Sorry, Mags, not quite done here. Freelandish contracts and all that; you know how it is. But, hey, at least you shouldn't have any trouble paying the bills for a while, right?"

Garret gave her what he hoped passed for an charming smile as he cupped his hand, moving it up and down in imitation of her weighty coin-purse gesture from before. She froze, then looked as though she were about to clobber him with her serving tray. Instead, she grabbed the service slate, jotted her next order in a furious flurry of cracks and screeches, loaded up the drinks from the service bar, and stormed off.

*Great,* thought Garret, *now my one and only friend in this godsforsaken byss-pit hates me. Perhaps she'll quit and I'll have naught but this primping peacock for company. Pock my life!*

Meanwhile, Daringsford had apparently finished perusing the contract and was reaching for the inkwell. "Seems all well and good to me," he said, "I never was really much for breaks and benefits anyhow. I should tell you of my time with Lord Ravenlocke's repertory company back in Medan. Now there was a boss with no sense of humor. Not some one you could break bread with like ol' Tokky."

"You don't say," Garret replied, glumly chipping ice into a tin shaker.

"Ah yes," he said, wiping and dipping the quill with a flourish before setting it to the parchment. "Many's the time Kade and I spent bemoaning work and women over pints of Yllgoni grog and oysters."

"I'm sure he – wait, what?" Garret nearly dropped the shaker in mid-shake.

"Grog and oysters," said Farian, scrawling his first name on the contract in an elaborate series of loops and squiggles. "No better place for oysters than the Yllgoni coast, let me tell you. Just ask Kade, he's the real connoisseur."

Garret slammed the shaker down on the bar and grabbed Farian's hand before the minstrel could jot a single letter of his family name.

"Kade can't eat oysters," he said, baring his teeth in a triumphant grin. "We got a shipment once and he broke out in hives just from handling the shells."

To his credit, the bard didn't miss a beat. "Oh, of course," he said. "I was thinking of some one else. No, *Kade* and I never ate oysters. I'd have the oysters and he'd get the Machi Machi Fish."

"Of course he did," said Garret as he grabbed the contract, pulling it out from under Farian's quill and turning the "n" of his surname into an unsightly scrawl. With practiced professionalism, he nullified the enchantment on the parchment by drizzling ink from its bottle in the shape of an X across the entire sheet and tearing it neatly in two.

"Sir!" the minstrel exclaimed, leaping to his feet and affecting an indignant pose. "I can assure you, my friend Kade *will* vouch for me. I shall speak to him when he returns, and mention your lack of professionalism to boot!"

"You know," said Garret, still smiling as he squared his shoulders and looked the bard straight in the eye, "I think I'd like to see that. Master Wallingtok should be returning within the hour. Pull up a stool. I'll pour you a pint."

"You mock me, sir. And anyway, I haven't any money."

"Oh, I wouldn't dream of charging a friend of 'ol Tokky's'. I'm sure since the two of you go way back he won't mind giving you one on the house. Just be sure to mention it to him when he comes in." Garret grabbed a tankard and turned toward the lager cask, just slowly enough to make the minstrel sweat.

"You know," the bard nearly shouted just as Garret reached for the tap, "I think I *shall* take that position at the Wand and Chalice. You just be sure my friend Kade know's it's *your* fault things didn't work out!"

"Yeah, I'll do that," said Garret as the minstrel turned on his heel and stalked out the door in a huff.

*And good riddance to you,* he thought. *Ye gods, could you imagine working with* that *kullbung? With all his pompous attitude and trollshest stories? Heh! Maybe I'll never work for a Medanite lord, but at least I don't have to tell elaborate half-truths to get folks to like me. Comes from the pride and satisfaction of doing honest work for a living, I suppose...*

"Master Stockwell!"

Garret jumped at Kade's voice in spite of himself. The dark, little man was standing by the service bar with a particularly sour expression on his thin face.

"I see you're deep in thought, *my friend.*" (Only Kade could make the term sound like an insult.) "Are you perhaps thinking of things more important than running my bar? This common room is a pigsty! I have some merchant bellowing about missing his business meeting, goblin children that are flinging bits of cheese at the rafters -- "

"Kade!" Maggie bounded up red-faced and huffing, sweat drenching her white blouse and leaving very little to the imagination. "Trina's not well. She's passed out in the washroom!"

"Well, get her out of there! It's bad for business!"

*Ah yes,* Garret thought as he barreled his way through a pack of screaming goblin children to get to the ladies' washroom, *pride and bloody, pocking satisfaction!*

## ~ II ~

*Muddlemogs! Naught but fog-witted, boot-snecking muddlemogs, the whole pocking lot of them!*

Farian Daringsford smoldered with contempt as he stood outside the grandest lecture hall of Angelwood University's Liepsbirgg School of Magic, and watched the constant flow of students bustling through its sandstone arches. They seemed an addled bunch, eyes unfocused, lips silently working as they bustled out of the building's flagstone paved vestibule, lost in private worlds of charged materia and graphoturgy. Or standing in clusters arguing heatedly over what metals and woods made the best fey loops and cast panels. Or slumped over on benches with stacks of spellbooks and ebony crystal cases, inspecting various devices and apparatuses, all with obscene amounts of joints, knobs, and lenses. All were dressed in fine silks and delicate featherflax linens exquisitely tailored into long dark coats or green-trimmed black cloaks in fashionable homage to the Lascivian mages they all aspired to become.

*Ten years!* he fumed. *Ten years in Lord Ravenlocke's Players. Two hundred stories. Three hundred songs on half a dozen different instruments. And these rich merchants' brats – these useless, vacky mongerspawn! – spend a few years, and a few thousand cenmarks learning illusions, and half the Freelands get dewy knickers over 'em!*

For the past two years the minstrel had gone from playhouse to playhouse, company to company, rejected time and again because he was not certified to work with Integrated Lascivian Magecraft ("ILM" as it was called by experienced Freelandish entertainers, or those that wished to appear as such). Problem was, there were only three ways to get ILM certification: enroll in a school of magic, spend several years doing grunt-work for slave's wages as a stagehand's apprentice, or bribe a director to vouch for you. At twenty-seven years, Farian knew he was too old for the first two options, which meant he would have to hustle up enough money for the third. And that, since Angelwood's service jobs were proving as competitive and closed to new talent as the rest of the polis, was proving to be no easy task.

Which brought him to this current, shall we say – venture?

Farian stood in a copse of olive trees far enough away from the lecture hall so as not to be noticed, but close enough for a clear view of every bespectacled face and finery-garbed frame. He leaned against a tree trunk, his casual posture belying the raptorial focus of his gaze, scanning the crowd, not for a student so much as a particular *type* of student.

And then he saw him – a nervous, pasty-faced fellow, standing slightly apart from the rest of the crowd. Farian could not say if it was the way the youth's flat, greasy hair stuck to his forehead that caught his interest, or the way his puffy lips twitched and double chin jiggled as he mentally reviewed his class notes, or the way he walked hunched over with shoulders tensed as though he expected the sky to fall on him at any moment. All he knew was that there was something about the young man's demeanor that made some turning gear hidden in the deepest part of his brain click and whirl, propelling him into action.

Farian followed the student across the campus, carefully staying just outside his field of vision, casually slinking from poplar hedge, to vine-covered pillar, to the far side of a statue of the legendary scholar-knight Benjin Nightshade, with his marble cloak swirling, iconic lantern held high. The minstrel moved with perfect poise and confidence, always exuding the air of an upright citizen with nothing to hide, going about his mundane and perfectly legitimate affairs. He had covered his hose and doublet with the simple, paint-and-clay-stained tunic and apron of a common laborer, so anyone he passed simply took him for one of the carpenters, masons, or bricklayers working on Nightshade Hall – a construction project so steeped in perpetual parchment shuffling, that the university had been stopping and restarting it for the better part of five years.

The student turned round the gray, stone corner of the college's library and onto a lonely walkway under the dense canopy of two rows of greatflower trees leading to the dormitories. Farian knew now was time to act. Without missing a step, he reached into his apron pockets and grabbed a pinch of clay dust with one hand, and a handfull of bloodcurrants in the other. In one motion, he threw the dust in his face and crushed the berries on his scalp just above his hair line.

"Meh-stah! Meh-stah!" he cried running at the student, and affecting the chopped, nasal accent of a Gimadran laborer. "Pees! Pees hehp! There been a hor'buh accident!"

The student took one look at Farian's chalk-covered, teary-eyed face streaked with streams of what appeared to be blood, and turned green. This was precisely the reaction Farian wanted.

"My fren'. He fah down. He hurt reeh bad. Pees come hehp us!"

"What happened?"

"Over at big bihding back dhere." Here waved back in the direction of the Nightshade Hall construction site.

"Look, I, uh - what do you need me to do?"

"Jus' – jus' hehp me fix. His arm – is like this, and bone like that. And his leg bone sticking out through skin like this. Is no too bad. Lots o' bhud. *Laaahts* o' bhud! But no too bad, yah?"

"Right. Lots of blood. Not too bad. Don't you think you should get a doctor? The physician's school is right over there."

"No! No doctah. Is too much money. Five gohd cenmarks. I have one, maybe two or three when my fren' wake up. We no get paid 'til next Arbiday. Now hlisten, when I put back hleg bone, he gon' scream reah hloud. What you do is – "

"L-look here, if it's a question of money, my parents sent me some gold for school supplies. Final projects aren't due for two months. I can put off buying my crystal kit – "

"No, no. You no need give money. I break finger once and fix. Arm and hleg same thing. Just bigger. And much more bhud."

"No! I mean, come now. Look at yourself, man! Covered in blood. Talking of b-broken bones! Just get a doctor. Please! You and your friend can pay me back after you get paid."

With doughy fingers trembling and shining with sweat, the student opened his purse, counted out three gold coins, and then thrust them in Farian's direction. The bard made a show of weighing his options before reaching out for the coins.

"Hey! You there! Stop! Don't give him any money!"

The student turned his slack-jawed face in the direction of the voice. Farian, however, did not. He knew the university stavemen had been watching for him ever since he'd begun plying his injured Gimadran laborer ploy two months prior. Instead he clasped the student's hand in both of his.

"Thank you, meh-stah! Thank you a hun'red time! I go now!"

The student turned back to him, confusion plain on his pasty features as he tried to work out what was happening. Before he could, however, the gold coins slipped from his sweaty fingers into Farian's hand, and the bard ran off, shouting broken platitudes and promises of repayment over his shoulder as he fled.

# The Centaur and the Sot

"Sir! Stop at once! We have you surrounded!"

*Benjin's baubles you do!* thought Farian, his boots flying over the cobbled walkway toward the wrought-iron gates at the edge of campus. *This school can't afford to fix half its facilities, let alone keep any more than the minimum number of stavemen. There's no way you'd have enough to – oh, pock!*

A line of no fewer than six stavemen assembled in front of the gateway, blocking his escape. Their black, boiled leather armor gleamed in the mid day sun as they held their smooth spindleoak quarterstaffs at alternating angles, forming an impenetrable phalanx. Farian skidded to a stop, nearly stumbling over the uneven cobblestones, and looked behind him. The staveman who'd shouted at him had been joined by two more running at either side of the walkway, hoping to intercept his flanks.

If he'd paused for even a second, they'd have caught him. But the minstrel, trusting instincts honed from over twenty years of narrow escapes, ran to the nearest building and leapt through the first doorway he saw. The doorway opened into a high-ceilinged foyer, which opened into a grand loggia with terracotta brick archways and weathered oak balustrades completely surrounding a festively decorated courtyard. Within the courtyard stood a dais where several men in scholarly robes seemed to be taking turns reading renowned poems and prose in various uninteresting ways, and a well-dressed crowd assembled to watch with feigned interest while servants (no doubt underclassmen paid in extra credit) passed out canapés and glasses of wine.

Without so much as a hitch to his stride, Farian jumped over the nearest balustrade and darted behind a large juniper bush before any of the partygoers could pay him any notice. As the sounds of stavemen clattering through the building's entryway grew in volume, he stripped off his workman's tunic and apron revealing his fine black and gold doublet and hose beneath. Then he grabbed a small flask from one of his apron's pockets, doused the inside of the tunic with water and scrubbed his face completely clean of bloodcurrant juice and clay. In seconds, the bard transformed himself from grubby laborer with a head wound to distinguished partygoer.

The stavemen filed into the courtyard and began pulling aside students and teachers for questioning. Farian grabbed an unattended beret and put it on his head while no one was paying attention. Then, thinking to further conceal his identity, he caught the attention of a stout, red-faced professor sporting a yellow and green striped houpelande, over sized sleeves flapping about his corpulent thighs, and started a conversation.

"I say, might I ask your name? I believe you helped my uncle on a research project."

"Oh-ho! Hum! Well, now, you're a Medanite if I ever saw one. You wouldn't be Thakeus Badgerfoot's nephew, would you?"

*I am now.*

"The very same! And, might I say, my uncle speaks fondly of you every time I cross his path. What was that old project you and he were working on, anyway?"

"Why, his thesis on *The Primrose and the Manticore*, of course."

"Of course! How could I forget?" said the bard, mentally sending a prayer of thanks to Mogu, the Medanite god of thieves and players that this was a gathering of *literary* academics, not alchemists, merchants, or mages. "But that's one of the most popular ballads in Medan. Surely Uncle Thakeus couldn't have written anything about it that hadn't been said a thousand times already."

"Bah! A common misconception, sure enough, but you see a story like this is so loaded with cultural significance its analysis could be approached from a hundred different angles. We actually – and here's the amazing thing – we actually found a much older version of the tale in the Solanische Warrior Sagas. Now your uncle – "

*-- was a drunkard whose oafishness was matched only by my father's,* thought Farian. Still, his disguise seemed to be working. As the portly academic hurled headlong into a flush-faced, sleeve-flapping soliloquy about the subtle stylistic

distinctions between Medanite and Solanische poetry, Farian feigned wide-eyed enthrallment as he kept the stavemen in his peripheral vision while they dispersed throughout the crowded courtyard. They moved delicately for men in armor, loathe to disrupt this gathering of well-to-do faculty and administrative officials.

Then someone grabbed his arm. Farian turned and found himself staring up into the scowling, square-jawed face of a staveman, his noseguarded, hardened leather helmet lending an excessive amount of gravity to his already stern features. In a voice clipped and hard as dwarven hammers on granite, he told the minstrel to come with him for questioning.

“By the Abyss!” the professor blustered. “What are you rock-mogged lackwits on about this time?”

"Dr. Vardamor, I'm sorry to interrupt. I just need to ask your friend here a few questions."

"Then ask, man! I've as much right to know your business with him as anyone. Seeing as how I'm on the committee that oversees the budget for your wages."

"Ah-ha, yes. You see, we were pursuing this vagabond who's been tricking students into giving him money. We saw him come through here – "

"Ridiculous! I've seen no such person, have you, dear boy?"

Farian responded with his best bewildered shrug.

"There, you see?" the professor continued. "There are no such vagabonds here. You and your men are just too lazy or incompetent to continue your pursuit."

"Sir, we have reason to believe our quarry might be assuming some sort of disguise. Your friend here is of the same height and build – "

"You think *this* young man is your *vagabond*? Outrageous! Why, do you even know who this is?"

"Sir, please remain calm. I only meant – "

"This young man's uncle is one of the premier voices in Mystican literary taxonomy! Not that I expect you or any of these other leatherheads to appreciate such things."

"So you're prepared to vouch for him, then?"

"But nooo, you'd rather disrupt poetry readings and harass your betters with base accusations – "

"Right. Come on, boys. He probably slipped out the back."

And with that, the staveman left, taking the better part of his cohorts with him and leaving Farian free and clear. Mostly. Four of the stavemen stayed behind, watching the garden party from various points about the surrounding loggia in case their fugitive revealed himself. So, to keep up appearances, Farian had to keep Doctor Vardamor talking until the event's conclusion at sunset. By the time the partygoers began to file out of the lantern-lit courtyard, the bard was rubbing his aching eyes and hoping he would never hear the terms "antithetical couplet" or "iambic pentameter" ever again.

*There must be an easier way to make a living,* Farian reflected, as he walked through the university's iron gates, fondling the purse on his belt, and feeling the muffled clinks of the three gold coins therein. Sure, three gold fenmarks were more than three month's pay for most in Angelwood in those days, but it was only half of what the most hard-up entertainments director would take as a bribe for an ILM voucher. And the gods alone knew from whence any more money would be coming. Now that the security officials at the college were keeping watch for him, it could take him months to find another goldmine of such gullible rich folks, if one existed at all.

*If the impresarios at The Pit would stop leading me on like a pheasant on Feastday and give me some regular stage time, I wouldn't have to hustle my marks like a common criminal,* he thought, wanting to spit.

Now he walked through the evening's gloaming, eastward from the university, down the broad expanse of newly refurbished cobblestone that was Hillrise Avenue. A blacksmith's hammer rang in the distance, its tones crisp and rhythmic as the ticks of a water-clock, setting the pace of the work day. Farian found himself, as he meandered, scanning the merchants as they vacated their offices and closed up their boutiques. There were men leaving cobblers and tailors wearing shiny leather aprons and boots. The only thing looking even slightly worn about their persons were the cases and satchels containing their shears, mallets, needles or some such assortment of craftsmen's tools that they'd no doubt had since their first days as journeymen. There were women, too. These seemed to come mostly from the dress shops and millineries, all adorned with the latest fashions of frilled dresses and broad-rimmed hats. Some of them waved to each other, exchanging banal pleasantries, but for the most part they kept to themselves, mentally running their personal circle-tracks of revenue projections and marketing schemes.

He scanned the crowds as he walked, checking every behavior for an opening, every face for that wide-eyed receptivity that no good dupe could go without for long. Instead he saw pursed lips, tense brows, and precise and methodical movements betokening pragmatic natures with no tolerance for the impulsive acts and delusions of grandeur that were every hustler's (and every minstrel's) stock and trade. At last he conceded that Hillrise Avenue, for all its finery and commerce, held nothing for the likes of him.

It wasn't until the last leg of his journey home, when he turned a corner onto Artisan Way, that he saw a face that caught his attention. It was the sharp-nosed, murine face of a dour little man with the body and bearing of a housecat climbing out of a tub of cold water. He was leaving a pristine, white building (now stained guttering orange as the last of daylight faded and the lamplighters finished their rounds) with smooth walls and clay moldings in sleek, sweeping lines that might have been better suited to a chariot than a center of business. Farian trailed the man for a full two blocks before he figured out where he'd seen him before. This was that annoying drunkard who'd insulted him a week prior when he'd nearly landed that barkeep job at the Dragonsbane Inn. And that was the very place, now that he noticed it, to which the dour little figure seemed to be returning tonight.

Now Farian could not say whether it was providence,

coincidence, or his own rapacious nature, but at that moment, the bard was seized with a strange predilection for the man's company. It was as though the drunkard were a bramble bush in fall, filled with luscious berries that the minstrel knew were his and his alone, if only he could find his way past the thorns. And so he followed the man - Stefan, he remembered his name had been - as he turned off Artisan Way and began his journey past the taverns, ether-houses, and bordellos of Angelwood Boulevard.

. When at last they reached the inn, the sounds of clacking wood, clinking tin, and slurred, raucous voices hit Farian in a warm rush along with the dancing glow of guttering oil lamps, and the swampy funk of ale-soaked floor-reeds. Stefan wended his way through the common room, and Farian followed, careful to keep his baring casual and just out of the drunkard's line of sight. They edged their way around a squat, circular table with four dwarves, all bellowing at each other at once in what could have either been a heated argument or some kind of celebration, hopped over the sprawled hooves of a pair of satyrs, drinking mead and eyeing barmaids as if each were their personal property, and ducked under the long, stiff, reptilian tail of an embalmed seraph hatchling that someone had partially dislodged from its perch in the rafters.

But for all the seedy chaos of the place, the thing Farian noticed most of all was the money. It swirled and flowed around him in coppery streams with silver sparkles. The concept of tipping was an unusual one in those days, unique to the Freelands and the more commercial provinces of the Gimadran Empire. Here in Angelwood, it was a custom to which tavern-goers quickly assimilated. A copper hawmark or cutmark would ensure your barmaid's timely return. A silver mark might win you a smile, a kiss or even a surreptitious fondle. Service without gratuity meant being ignored, humiliated, and, if someone told the nearest staveman of your miserliness, in serious danger of waking the next day penniless and stuffed into a sewage canal. Farian watched with admiration as the wenches plied their trade, and the tide of currency poured from the customers' purses into cash boxes and apron pockets all wending its way about the room to arrive at the epicenter of it all: the barkeep.

*Ah, the coin I could win with such a job!* the minstrel mused. *Charming the women, baiting the men, and all the while getting them too soused to notice the increasing lightness of their purses. I could do great things with such a job, great things indeed!*

The bar was as Farian remembered – a simple, boxy structure with a dozen rickety stools before it and a dimly lit, though well-ordered, space behind. Still following Stefan, he watched the rat-faced little drunkard heft himself onto the nearest barstool with a great deal of grousing and grumbling (from both him and the stool) and wave to the barkeep. To Farian's relief, the man behind the bar was not the same beefy, bald fellow who had all but thrown him out the week before, but was instead a thin man with black hair in thick spidery locks, a wide toothy grin, and skin so dark it was almost the color of soot.

*A Rialtran,* Farian noted, taking an empty stool beside Stefan. *Never saw too many of his folk back in Medan. Or anywhere else for that matter. Gods, I love the Freelands!*

"Triple shushang. Neat."

"Nice to see you again, too, Stefan." The Rialtran barkeep had a rich gravelly voice, and his full lips moved around the words in a way that seemed almost like chewing. "An' will you be checking the menu this ev'ning? Or maybe your tab?"

"Bah," said Stefan. "It's only Favaday, it can't be *that* high yet. An' don't give me too much shest tonight, B'lahn, it's been *that* kind of a day."

"I hear you there, friend," he gave the dour, little man a big, bright smile as he poured his whiskey, then looked at Farian and gave him a welcoming nod.

The bard fingered the three gold coins in his purse trying to do a brief calculation of how he would budget them out over the next month. He gave up halfway through, and slammed one down on the bar with a grin.

"A mug of your darkest and finest, please."

B'lahn the barkeep took the coin with a raised eyebrow and a barely noticeable glance around the place to see if any of the inn's less savory patrons had noticed the glint of gold, before grabbing a tankard and moving to a rack of hogshead casks by the back counter. Stefan, for his part, seemed uninterested in any gold save the glimmers dancing in his whiskey glass and paid the exchange no mind whatsoever.

"I say, fellow, haven't I seen you somewhere before?" Farian approached Stefan with his usual opening line for striking up conversations with total strangers. The barkeep gave him a tankard of brown ale, and a dubious look before turning to the lockbox to count out the minstrel's change. Stefan, in response to the minstrel's query, gave Farian a squinty-eyed once-over, then muttered something unintelligible and turned back to his drink.

"No, really," Farian pressed, "I'm positive I know you. And from somewhere really important, too. What do you do for a living?"

Stefan snorted derisively into his tilted glass.

"If you don't mind me asking."

"What do I do?" said the sot, after a just-long-enough-to-be-uncomfortable pause. "Take it up the kull-bung like a hawmark whore in Gimmi-town, that's what I do! An' I'm paid about as much to do it, too. Ya wanna know what's wrong with the world today?"

And with that, Stefan launched into a slurred, bar-pounding, spittle-spraying diatribe about his obtuse bosses at Whyte and Golde Building Company, his obstinate client, a centaur horse-trader with more temper than common sense, and various uncomfortable-sounding sexual acts they could all do to each other. As the drunkard's rant grew less coherent, expanding in scope to include indictments against stavemen, elvish snobs from Bentwood, and women who put too much olive oil in their hair, Farian's smile became more and more forced. He glanced at B'lahn, who gave him a sympathetic look but made sure to stay at the other end of the bar. What *had* he gotten himself into?

"So you're a builder, then," said Farian, the moment Stefan paused for a swallow of liquor. "A contract clerk perhaps, or a foreman?"

"Master planner," he muttered, then noticing Farian's shocked expression, expounded with a dismissive wave of his hand, "My brother-in-law's on the polis council. Pulled a few strings. Got me a few promotions more than I should've had. You know how it is in this town."

He trailed off, and after another swallow of whiskey, launched into another incoherent rant in which the bard could discern little more than the phrase "horse-pocking centaur" used repeatedly and with great emphasis.

*What am I even doing here?* thought Farian to himself. *Listening to this lush. A master planner no less! Sweet Mogu, remind me to avoid entering any of* those *buildings not wearing plate mail!*

Yet still, there was something about the situation that kept his attention: a small voice in the stillest, darkest point in the center of the bard's ever-swirling whirlwind of mental activity that said, "Wait. Look. Listen. There is something here that you can use." Perhaps it came from instincts honed by a lifetime of hard living. Perhaps it was the voice of Mogu himself. Either way, it was that same voice that had guided him through many a precarious predicament in the past, and Farian knew better than to ignore it.

"So you've a centaur for a client?" he blurted, latching on to the last cogent malison to burble from the drunkard's driveling mouth.

Stefan had to take a moment to mentally review the progression of his tirade (Which by now had moved on to how his brother-in-law and the rest of the polis council were apparently conspiring to take away his job because he was wise to all their shady backroom deals.) before nodding his assent.

"Aye, that's right, a centaur. An' a right ornery pockstocker he is, too."

From there, Stefan regaled the minstrel with an account of how the centaur horse-trader, one Radamir Loradwn, had hired the master builder to construct a trade post in Angelwood a few blocks to the east on the corner of Aurora Boulevard and Hills Pass. At first, the centaur had been brimming with grandiose schemes of multi-tiered stables and marble-floored showrooms. Then, when the invoices began rolling in for all the imported building materials, along with the numerous unforeseeable tariffs and fees imposed by the notoriously fickle Freelandish Alliance of Merchants, the horse trader grew surly and tightfisted even to the point of accusing the merchant guilds of taking advantage of him (which, in all fairness, they probably were). Now, Master Loradwn was insisting that Stefan find a way to design for him the trading post of his dreams with half the necessary materials, at a fraction of the cost. What was more, any attempted negotiation on the part of the master planner was met with bellowed accusations and threats of bodily dismemberment.

"Hmm," said Farian, nodding sympathetically, "shouldn't take those threats lightly either. I knew more than a few centaurs back in Medan. Proud folks, and dumb as the beasts they resemble in matters of art, business, and civilized society. But try to tell *them* any of that and ho, boyo! They'll be picking parts of you out of the trees!"

"See!" cried Stefan. "You know what 'm talkin' about! You don't know anything about centaur architecture, do you?"

And with that, the final pieces of the scheme swirling about in Farian's head fell into place.

"But of course, my friend. As it so happens, I was building planner back in Medan. That's where I know *you* from. Not Medan, but that last big Builder's Guild function – social, thingy."

"You mean the Builder's Convention last spring?"

"Yes. That. Exactly. I happen to be a journeyman of some talent *and* an expert when it comes to centaur society (Or what passes for it, right? Hahahahaha!). Do you have your plans with you? If we can get a table, I can help you right now."

Stefan's face lit up with weepy-eyed gratitude as he

enthusiastically thanked the bard, and clasped his wrist in a vigorous, shoulder-popping handshake. Farian spied a small round table by the kitchen doorway and the two of them made their way through the churning sea of patrons, Stefan clutching his drink in one hand while he fumbled with the endcap of a cylindrical chart-case with the other.

Now Farian, of course, knew as much about architecture as he did of sword-fighting, seraph-riding, or spectacular graphoturgy, which is to say, nothing at all. But he found with Stefan, as he had countless times before, that ignorance can be easily masked with flattery, a cool temperament, and a lot of intelligent-sounding questions. "Well, how would *you* create the illusion of lightness in a load-bearing wall?" he would say, or "Oh sir, I'm sure a man of your expertise has a much keener grasp of negative space ratios than I."

The bard did, however, happen to know quite a lot about centaurs. Farian's home country of Medan was bordered to the southwest by the predominantly centauran and faunish nation of Robystern. He remembered his father, descendant of nobility brought low by ill-favored investment to the profession of a scholar, and lower still by self-loathing and drink. For some years the only work the man could procure was tutoring centauran immigrants, and some of the few happy memories from Farian's childhood involved playing with and even riding some of their coltish younglings. That was until his father abandoned his family when Farian was twelve to join a merchant caravan, of course, but that was another story.

Paternal resentment notwithstanding, Farian remembered that centaurs, particularly immigrants, were mistrustful and extremely hot-tempered when they thought they were being taken advantage of. As they were a people coming from a country where the closest thing to a city was little more than three-score barn-like long-houses scattered around a prairie, these fears proved well-founded far too often. So, as Stefan took Farian deeper and deeper into his confidence (while imbibing dose after dose of shushang), the bard managed to sell the boozehound builder on a number of cost-cutting ideas. And these ideas, if the minstrel's memories served him right, would elicit just the right sort of response from Stefan's client. Farian only hoped the pathetic little sot could sort out all the last-minute modifications they were making to his plans in the sobering light of day tomorrow.

There was one point in particular Farian knew he had to make abundantly clear. "Now write this down so you don't forget," he said, gripping Stefan by his narrow shoulders and looking him straight in his dazed, watery eyes. "Centaurs are at their most ornery in offices or human places of commerce. So don't discuss any of these new proposals at your workplace. Set up a lunchtime meeting, and bring him here."

"Here? Y'mean the Dragonsbane? Ahh..." Stefan nodded sagaciously. "Y'mean, keep things in a friendly environment an' such. Show 'im there's nothing to be afraid of."

*For* him, *anyway,* Farian thought, as he fixed the master builder with his winningest smile and raised his tankard. "Precisely. To success in business."

Stefan's whisky glass tunked against the tankard's wooden rim, and he downed a mighty gulp of shushang as though it were nothing at all. Farian, on the other hand sipped his ale slowly. He intended to retire early tonight. After all, whether this long-shot plan of his worked or not, tomorrow would be an interesting day indeed.

## ~ III ~

As fate or Mogu willed it, the next day found the Dragonsbane Inn busier than it had been in years. Today was The Pit's seventh annual Glories of Battle Parade, held to celebrate (and more importantly, promote) the arena's pugilistic performers. By mid-afternoon, countless varieties of gladiators, singers, and entertainers of all kinds would stomp, tumble, and drum their way down Anglewood Boulevard, and the boardwalks, lots, and patios lining the cobblestoned thoroughfare seethed with jam-packed masses, churning in anticipation. By an hour past midday, every tavern, restaurant, and tea-house on the street had filled well past maximum capacity with rowdy Pit-fight fanatics sporting costume armor and waving fake weapons and wooden facsimiles of severed limbs.

Farian sat on a stool at an overturned ale barrel, hastily wedged between two window-side tables. If he craned his neck forward he could get a distorted view of the crowded porch through the grime-tinted, diamond shaped panes of age-warped glass, but nothing of the street beyond. At the table in front of him, four young dock workers from Long Bay argued boisterously about which Pit performer would eviscerate whom, while at his back a finely dressed elvish couple from

Beaver Tree Hill complained about the inferior quality of their seedcakes and wine.

But Farian was not there for the view. At least not that of the parade. From his unobtrusive vantage he could scan the milling crowds of the common room for Stefan, or rather the building planner's client. For while the man's slight build and unremarkable appearance would make him all but impossible to pick out in such a crowd, it would be quite hard to overlook a centaur.

"Sir, can I fetch you anything?"

Farian started to wave the barmaid away, then reconsidered when he noticed just how, well, *fetching* the girl actually was. She had a dazzling blue-eyed smile and golden hair tied back with a strip of gauzy, blue-green fabric too thick to be a ribbon, but too small to be a scarf. Her only blemish was a slight bump and fading shadow of a bruise on her right temple that, to Farian, only made her more intriguing. He met her eyes and gave her a dazzling smile of his own.

"Something light in a tall mug. I may be here a while. Though I do hope that won't inconvenience the throngs of people clamoring for such a luxurious table." He patted the side of the wine barrel.

"You'd be surprised on a parade day. Maggie says a man once paid silver so he could sit on the front stairs. Say, is that a lute case?"

"It is." Farian grabbed the case from where he'd wedged it between the barrel and the wall and pulled it onto his lap. More out of reflex than anything else, he removed the instrument and slid the case behind him with one hand while grabbing the neck and allowing the belly to plop onto its long-accustomed place on his left thigh.

"I'm still fairly new to the area," he said, making small talk as he tuned his strings, "so I haven't found a regular place to play. I was just planning on finding a street corner somewhere after I'm done here."

"Well, watch out for the stavemen. Most street corners in this town are owned by merchants. They'll just give you a warning most of the time, but once in a while they'll fine you for loitering."

"Figures," Farian sighed, "and with most of the inns, taverns and etherhouses booked solid with their favorite performers, such a meandering melodist as I has nary a chance at honest work. You'd think a place like Angelwood, legendary haven for artists and entertainers, would be a bit more receptive to new talent."

"Gods, you really haven't been here long, have you?" the barmaid laughed. "Minstrels here would cast a sunder hex on their sweet Aunt Ivy for even an *hour* of stage time."

"And you're a performer of some sort yourself, I suppose."

"No. I just have... a thing for musicians."

Something about the girlish way that she said it inspired Farian to play then. Because it was still fresh in his mind after his caper at the university the day before, he played a verse from The Primrose and the Manticore.

> "The fairy maiden, Primrose, saw
> the knight was grim and sore.
> And fearsome as the battered sigil
> all his brethren bore.
> She wondered then how e'er she'd bear
> This vicious Manticore."

The barmaid gave a theatrical groan and rolled her eyes. It was not the reaction Farian usually got to the romantic ballad.

"Truly? You couldn't think of anything less maudlin? Star-crossed lovers overcome their differences and come together only to be torn apart when winter comes. What dref!"

"It was the first thing that came to mind. Perhaps you'd prefer to hear one about Jeni Tynsaryl and her silver arrows, or Susa the Ogres' Daughter."

"Perhaps another time. The barkeep's giving me dirty looks so I should probably get back to my other tables. It was nice meeting you, Master..."

"Daringsford. Farian Daringsford."

"And I'm Trina UiConnal. I'll be right back with your ale, Master Daringsford."

He watched her a while as she checked on other tables and made her way back to the bar. *Yet another potential perk of tavern work*, he mused, admiring the way the barmaid twisted and swayed her way through the crowded common room. *A girl like that could really light a fire in your lyre. Young, trim, and witty to boot. And, oh, the things I would do to that wonderful little kull!*

As Farian lifted his eyes from Trina's retreating posterior, however, he caught the eye of the barkeep and almost jumped out of his skin. It was that same bald, beefy fellow who'd torn up his employment contract the week before. And not only that, but he was holding his ice-pick and staring at him with a baleful glare, as though trying to think of an excuse to use it.

*Oh, come now, don't be freppish. There's no reason he'd bear me* that *much ire. I was just trying to get a job, after all, using my natural talents just like any other –*

Then the barmaid, Trina, approached the bar to give the fellow her drink order and the barkeep's expression brightened as suddenly as flash pot in a darkened theater. His dark eyes sparkled, his bald pate flushed, his scruffy goateed mouth split into a goofy, double-rowed grin, and Farian immediately knew why he had made the man so irate. Cursing his bad luck, the minstrel vowed to himself that he would keep his irresistible powers of seduction in check until *after* he'd seen his latest ploy for employment through to the end.

And speaking of which...

An emanation of irritated muttering and shoving swelled outward through the crowd clustered at the inn's entryway as a centaur - one Radamir Loradwn by Farian's estimation - eased his way into the common room. He was an imposing fellow, his equine hinder-half a shimmering black with flecks of gray, and about three-quarters the size of a thoroughbred stallion. His human parts were impressive as well, with hints of hard muscle contained snugly beneath a doublet that was a finely crafted blend of earth tones and emeralds, along with a coifed van dyke and a luxuriant head of black and grey hair, the same color as his flanks. He held himself with all the pride and dignity of a successful merchant, broken only by a fierce glare shot at a bellowing dwarf whose foot had the audacity to slip beneath his falling back hoof.

As for Stefan the master planner, his entrance proved a less impressive spectacle. He hopped about his client like a nervous flea, trying to sweet talk the centaur, placate the irritated patrons around him, and flag down a serving wench all at the same time. As Farian watched a flushed and breathless serving girl lead the two on a long, contorted journey through the crowd to their table, he supposed it was fortunate that Stefan had thought to reserve the table before leaving last night. Unfortunately the old sot had neglected to mention (and Farian had neglected to remind him) that his lunchtime companion would be a centaur, and require at least three times the amount of room as the inn's usual variety of guest. So Master Loradwn, after having to sidle his way delicately through the common room, was lead to a table in the corner only slightly higher than his knees where he would have to twist his torso sideways to keep his tail out of the stew bowls of the party beside them.

Trina plunked a tankard of ale onto the barrelhead, and Farian gave her a full silver mark as payment with a wave signifying she should keep the change. Then, as the barmaid graced him with a beaming smile for his generosity, he asked if Master Wallingtok was about. Immediately her smile dropped.

"Yes, I suppose he is," she said, her look equal parts perplexity and repugnance. "What do you want with him ?"

"You might want to tell him to keep an eye on that centaur. He has the look of one who's ready to start chucking buckets at any moment."

"Really?" Trina glanced skeptically at the visibly irritated but still quite composed Radamir Loradwn.

"Trust me, I know trouble when I see it."

"Okay..." the barmaid shrugged and turned toward the kitchen to go find her boss. Farian waited until she was a decent distance away, then took a long belt of ale before rising and making his way toward Stefan and the centaur's table. He sauntered casually, making a show of admiring the artifacts and stuffed creatures decorating the room, and always careful to stay out of the master planner's line of sight. Soon he was close enough to pick their conversation out of the din of the other patrons.

"I really don't have time for this," Loradwn was saying, his voice the low rumble of a distant thunderstorm. "If we're going to look at building plans, wouldn't your office be more appropriate?"

"Nonsense!" said Stefan, contorting his scrawny arms every which way as he tried to open his parchment tube in the narrow confines of the booth. "I know how you people feel ill at ease in places of business, so I brought you here: my home away from home!"

"Ill at ease? You do realize I *am* a *businessman*, right? And what do you mean, 'you people'?"

"Why, centaurs, of course. People of the Hoof, Runners of the Fields, favored children of Rastwyn the Swift," Stefan beamed with pride at his newfound worldliness, oblivious to the centaur's narrowing eyes. "I did some research last night."

"Did you, now?"

"Yes. And I think I've found the perfect way–" Stefan pulled his building plans out of their case and flung them onto the table knocking his whiskey glass onto the floor in the process. "—to solve our little funding and materials problem. Not to mention accommodate certain cultural indulgences at the same time, eh?"

Stefan winked at the centaur, to which the merchant responded with a look of utter confusion. But the builder was too busy poring over his plans to notice.

"See, the stalls that go here have an ingenious design with an entrance to the front and the rear, so you can—"

"Wait, what am I looking at here, my offices or the

stables?"

"Both!"

Farian couldn't be sure with the crowd and the dim lighting, but he was fairly certain he could see the hairs on the centaurs beard actually stand on end as he fixed the rat-faced little man with a black-eyed stare.

"You put my offices – in with the *horses*?"

"Isn't it wonderful?" Stefan prattled on, oblivious to the merchant's growing furor. "Now as I was saying, these stalls have gates in the front and the rear, so—"

"And why in the Great pocking Abyss would I ever want a gate to the rear of a horse?"

"Well, er, you know – because of your culture's special (ahem!) relations they, I mean you – would have with the—"

"What *are* you burbling about?"

"Look, friend, it's no great controversy, really. I mean, what you do behind closed doors is none of my concern. I mean, pock me 'til my stalk drops off, this *is* the Freelands after all, and any carnal proclivities a man might – or centaur rather..."

Farian watched the merchant carefully as he glowered at Stefan's stammering, getting more perplexed and more irate by the minute. Then in one glorious instant the minstrel saw the centaur jerk backwards as though the revelation of the master planner's implications had struck him like a crossbow bolt to the chest.

"Are you saying that I have *sex* with my *horses*?"

For an awkward instant that seemed an eternity, Stefan's mouth worked like that of a suffocating fish as he struggled to come to grips with his client's unanticipated reaction.

*He could still mend things,* Farian realized, grinding his teeth in anticipation. *Loradwn looks more shocked than offended. All the little bugger needs to do is explain that he got some bad information. Then he could smooth things over, postpone the project a little longer; the sot goes back to his drawing board, the centaur back to his business, and I go back to the streets with nearly a full day's hustling wasted!*

But instead Stefan said, "Well, don't you?"

The centaur's fist slammed into the table with a resonant crack, as every patron in the crowded inn turned to gape at the furious merchant. Loradwn, oblivious to their attention, stamped his hooves, heaved his massive chest and contorted his fierce, flushed features as he struggled to contain his rage.

"You – insolent – bigoted, little – kullbung!"

"Whoa! Now, see here, old clopper—"

Farian dropped to the floor as the massive table flew at him, tumbling in a torrent of splintered cherry wood to crash through the adjacent window. As he pushed himself up, soggy reeds staining and sticking to his hands, he saw the centaur clamp one massive hand around Stefan's forearm and another around his neck. The master builder went wide-eyed, struggling and squeaking in panic. All around them, chairs clattered, boots stomped and voices babbled in an incoherent roar as customers bolted from their tables to press themselves toward the walls of the common room, if not run out the door entirely.

Two burly figures in black leather plate – the house stavemen, no doubt; no Freelandish business could thrive without them – rushed the centaur from behind, quarterstaffs discarded in favor of smooth shiny cudgels for indoor peacekeeping. Without even turning, the centaur released Stefan's neck, and swatted one of the guardsmen with the back of his hand. The man's head snapped back sending his helmet spinning through the air before Loradwn grabbed his entire head in one hand and smacked it into the nearest post.

The second staveman did not even last that long. As soon as he was close enough, the beastly merchant mule-kicked him below his gut with his hind hoof, shattering his pelvis and sending him to the floor in a crumbled heap.

"Peace of the wind, friend! Peace of the wind!"

Farian shouted the words as only a bard can shout, clear tones cutting through room's chaotic din. The centaur, ham-sized fist still clutching Stefan's forearm, turned to regard the minstrel. The merchant's black-bearded face twisted and contorted, confusion disrupting his maddened rampage.

"What?" he spat.

"May the peace of the wind on your hair raise your passions and heal your heart, my friend," said Farian. The ancient blessing sounded odd here in this inn, so far away from the fields of southern Medan where the minstrel had played with centaur colts as a youth.

"Who the pock are you, and what makes you think you know one nut in a shest bucket about goes on here?"

The merchant released Stefan, who, if he had not been paralyzed with terror and confusion, might have bolted for the door then and there, and turned to face the bard. His face, while more composed than it had been, was still flushed with rage, and the stamping of his hooves as he repositioned himself caused the floor to shake.

"The master planner is a friend of mine."

"Is that so?"

Loradwn's dark eyes gleamed viciously as Farian crossed the floor to meet him. The minstrel could have placated the centaur then, as most probably would have done in his place: pleading and groveling in a pathetic attempt to soothe the imposing beast into complacency. Instead, the bard made a show of straightening his garments, running a hand through his hair, and dusting off bits of floor reeds from his doublet, saying not a word until he was just the right distance for the semi-equine merchant to reach out and rip off one of his arms if he so chose.

*And thus, does the heroic would-be barkeep put himself in harm's way for the sake of the inn,* he thought. He hoped the barmaid had gone to Wallingtok, and the proprietor was watching all this, but dared not take his eyes off the centaur long enough to look.

"We discussed your project last night," said Farian, "over a few drinks. A few too many, I fear, as Stefan here seems to have gotten everything I told him of Centauric culture entirely backwards."

"But didn't you say—" Stefan sputtered.

"The *stables,*" Farian pressed on, silencing the flustered

master builder with a look, "were *not* intended to appeal to some woefully inaccurate perception of your proud race. They were simply meant to maximize resources, and—"

"Con a dumb *clopper* out of his money?"

"Of course not!"

"Right." Loradwn smiled, displaying two rows of gleaming white teeth, and no good humor whatsoever. "But you did teach him that word, did you not? Clopper. And just what, I wonder, did you tell him it meant?"

"You said it was a term of endearment," Stefan hissed in an all too audible whisper.

Farian elbowed the old sot in the gut.

"De*file*ment, Stefan. I said it was a term of defilement and should never be—"

"Did you happen to mention," Loradwn grated, leaning over until Farian could count the number of gray whiskers in his beard, "the three hundred years of oppression, when Medanite slavers sold thousands of my kin like common cattle to plow their fields and build their cities?"

*Damn*, thought Farian, *I* thought *that expression might prove a bit too incendiary.*

"Well, I certainly told him not to—"

"You had no right!" the centaur roared. An enormous hand clamped around Farian's neck and lifted him into the air as easily as a chicken picked for slaughter. "That's *our* word, understand! You don't get to use it! Until your kind knows what it's like to be beaten and enslaved and used like *things*, that word has no business coming out of your stupid, human mouth!"

The monstrous merchant shook him as he bellowed. Farian felt his face tighten and swell, and his limbs flop about like those of a deflated wind puppet.

"Sorry," he forced through his strangled windpipe. "Meant – no offense. Trying to – save you money."

"Bones, you were! The pair of you were trying to save your*selves* money by cheating me out of my office space!"

"Not materials," he choked. "Taxes. Polis council.

New tax on—"

The room spun as Farian's vision faded into a black blur filled with tiny flashing lights. *I'm dying*, he thought. *Sweet Mogu, not like this! I've never sang in the grand arena of the Pit, never been to a fairy orgy at First Harvest, never worn a tunic of Syndraxan silk...*

When he felt the floor under his kicking heels, he thought it was only a hallucination of his air-deprived brain. Then suddenly he was standing, or at least trying so to do as his trembling legs threatened to buckle beneath him. Slowly, the gigantic hand unwrapped from around his neck, and he gasped, the scene around him fading in and out of focus as he fought to keep from collapsing in a fit of coughs.

"What do you mean 'taxes'?" said the centaur.

"The polis—" and here, the sound grated through his crumpled voice box and Farian had to double over coughing for a good long time, while Loradwn glared at him.

"Polis council passed a new tax," he finally forced out.

*My voice! Ye gods, I sound like a marsh troll coming out of hibernation. Oh Mogu, please let this idiotic plan not have cost me my beautiful singing voice!*

"When it takes affect, businesses will be taxed based on the number of their offices. With Stefan's design, you can claim your office is a stable and avoid the tax entirely."

"Trollshest! I've been tracking polis laws and regulations for over a year, and I never heard of any such tax."

"That's because it was a backroom deal. Someone misappropriated funds on the Angelwood River project or some such nonsense, and they needed a way to raise revenue fast. I wouldn't have known about it either if Stefan's brother-in-law weren't actually on the council."

The centaur opened his mouth as though for an angry retort, then closed it again as anger faded into bewilderment in his fierce, dark features.

"Well, hmm. That does *sound* like something the council might do."

"Look, you don't have to take my word for it. Go to the

polis municipium and talk to Stefan's brother-in-law. He has an accommodating character and a relatively clean slate tomorrow, and I'm sure he could make time for any matters regarding family members and their projects. At least that's what he told me when I talked to him this morning."

"I might just do that."

"Fine! And when you're satisfied you can stop by Stefan's office and go over his ingenious plans for your place of business like civilized adults. After I correct some of his misunderstandings about your most estimable culture, of course."

"Right," said the centaur. His fiery glare dropped into a pensive frown. He seemed more self-conscious now, as though Farian's self-confidence were eclipsing his own. "And just what is *your* stake in the matter anyhow?"

"If you must know," the bard retorted, "I was hoping to impress you. I'm a salesman by trade and I've been looking for work since my last employer went bankrupt. When my new friend Stefan mentioned his project to me last night and that the esteemed horse-merchant Radamir Loradwn was setting up shop here in Angelwood, I jumped at the chance to make your acquaintance and maybe apply for a place on your sales staff. Athough now—" here he paused, rubbing his bruised neck for emphasis.

"Ah-ha, yes. Well, that plan didn't work out too well for either of us then, did it?" Loradwn looked embarrassed as he shifted on his hooves. "Look, if you're still interested, I have an office on the corner of Hillrise Avenue and Tar Street. Assuming your story about the new tax checks out, I'll probably move ahead on my construction plans, after which I'll need all the clever new salesmen I can find."

"Assuming I survive the experience."

"Yes, well, sorry about that."

"Not a drop, friend. Think nothing of it. And I'm sorry about the whole c-word misunderstanding."

"As you say, not a drop."

And with that, the centaur made his awkward goodbyes

as he edged his way out the door. There was a breathless pause as the sound of hooves clopping on cobblestones faded into the muted clamor of the hide drums and trumpets in the passing parade outside. Then the room erupted into a frantic gabble of incredulous exclamations and elated tittering. Several of the inn's guests stumbled over each other to praise Farian for the exemplary way he handled the tense situation (although none of them had any clue as to how the "situation" actually started), while the barmaids and dappers scrambled about to help the injured and clean up the shattered furniture. One could tell by their quiet efficiency that most had performed such tasks many times before.

"I gotta tell ya," said Stefan, wedging himself through the press of giddy patrons and clasping Farian's hand. "That was amazing what you just did. Absolutely amazing! I couldn't follow half the hogs fodder you were feeding that monster, but you sure saved my sorry bone-sack, I'll tell ya what!"

"Don't mention it."

"I don't know how I got so mixed up about all those things you told me last night."

"Drink does funny things to a man's mog."

"That it does, friend. That it does. I tell ya, I'm about ready to give up the juice entirely after that little debauchery."

"I think you mean 'debacle'."

"That too."

Farian turned to see if his seat between the two front windows was still available. It was, although one of the windows had been smashed out by a flying cherrywood table that was now gods-knew-where in the street beyond. He was pleased to find, however, that not only was his tankard of ale seemingly untouched by the wreckage, but the persnickety elvish couple that had been seated behind him had understandably left the building. Farian grabbed his tankard, brushed the glass shards and splinters off the elves' former table and happily took a seat to enjoy a remarkable view of the passing parade. Stefan, still prattling on, plunked down into the seat across from him as though they were the best of pals.

"You've got a real gift with words, you know that? And the way you kept your poise with that great beast bearing down on you? A real gift! You should be a performer of some kind, you know?"

"The thought has crossed my mind once or twice."

"And how you told him about that tax – when *did* you meet my brother in law anyway?"

"Never. I made the whole thing up."

"Ha! But, wait, that means—" Stefan's face fell as realization slowly dawned on him, "when he goes to vilify your story—"

"*Verify*, Stefan. And yes, you *will* want to talk to your brother in law as soon as possible. Get him to write up a bill or proposal, whatever the local government uses to get things done around here. Just as long as it looks official."

"But we haven't spoken in years!"

"Well, rekindle the relationship then. Gods and demons, Stefan, do I have to do *everything*?"

"But I – and he – . Oh, pock me, this is bad! *Pock meee!*"

Stefan bolted for the door, hurdling chairs and slaloming tables as spryly as any of the Pit's acrobats doing synchronized somersaults down the boulevard outside.

*Hope he gets to the polis municipium before that centaur does*, thought Farian as he gazed out the shattered window. *I should be more concerned, but the air feels so good right now.*

Angelwood's climate was semi-arid, giving the polis fair, sunny weather for most of the year, and today was no exception. As the breeze tossed his hair, warm and playful as a maiden's fingers, he watched as the tumbling acrobats were replaced by a regiment of horn-players, their blaring, rhythmic tones celebrating the joyous, cheering chaos around them. He sipped his ale.

Soon enough, a staveman took the seat across from him and began asking him questions about the fight. Farian, having talked to his fair share of the polis' contracted guardsmen, answered his questions wearing his most guileless of grins. By the time the bard had finished his ale and ordered another, the staveman was smiling and bidding him good day as he took down the minstrel's address (which a rare an oh-so-innocent slip of the tongue on Farian's part rendered completely inaccurate).

*Ah well, at least Master Loradwn doesn't have my contact information either. Not like ol' Stefan. Poor little sot. Maybe I'll buy him a drink or three when I find steady work. If he's still got arms attached with which to hold it, that is.*

"Excuse me, young sir."

Farian turned to see a small, dark-skinned man wearing the wrapped cloth cap of an Yllgoni that could only be Kade Wallingtok.

"I understand that you were most helpful in the saving of my inn. Well, most of it anyway." He looked at the broken window distastefully.

"At least it happened after the rainy season."

"Indeed. Perhaps I should be taking the other one out to make it match. Might be good for business when the days get hot," he stared at the front of his inn for a while before shaking his head and taking the seat across from Farian. "But that is another matter entirely. I am wondering, young sir, what it is you are doing for a living?"

"Well Master Wallingtok, I'll tell you what I'd *like* to do."

From there Farian told the innkeeper about his goal of becoming a barkeep. He explained how his quick wits and skill with the public – as Kade had seen firsthand in his treatment of that fearsome centaur – made him an ideal candidate for the profession. Wallingtok took it all in with an unreadable frown that would have put most applicants on edge. Farian, however, was not intimidated in the least. The innkeeper, after all, was much too small to pick the minstrel up by the neck and, as far as Farian could tell, did not have any hooves.

# ~ IV ~

"Well, Master Stockwell, that was some quick thinking on your part. I think you may have missed your calling in keeping the peace or medicine!"

Garret shrugged in response, his nonchalance belied by his wide grin and flushed, shiny scalp. While the centaur and the minstrel had been locked in their dramatic exchange of placation and throttling, the master barkeep had told Ardeen, his second, to watch the bar, while he pulled three dappers away from their tables and rushed to the aid of the fallen stavemen. Hunched and wary of flying hooves, fists, or cherrywood tables, they had dragged the injured men to a clear section of floor in the back of the common room and surrounded them with a barricade of overturned chairs and benches. Garret's actions were only what came natural after years of breaking up fights and keeping drunkards more or less on their feet, but hearing the words of praise from the staveman inquisitor was a rare and wonderful treat.

"We're taking a statement from one of the people involved right now," the officer continued. He jerked his black-helmed head back and to the side, and Garret followed the gesture to see another guardsman sitting at a window-side table with a certain annoying minstrel the barkeep had been seeing entirely too much of lately. "Is there anything you can tell me about him we should know?"

*That he's a bosky, lying popinjay who thinks all of Ardyn should shower him with praise and riches for his every belch and kull-burp.*

"Don't know him that well. He's been here once or twice, but I couldn't tell you the first thing about him."

The staveman nodded and jotted some notes on a small piece of parchment with a charcoal-tipped stylus. Garret didn't know why he couldn't bring himself to mention the bard's fraudulent interview the week before. Perhaps he'd lived in Angelwood long enough to realize nearly everyone in the polis had one or two scams they were working at any given time. Or perhaps it was the euphoria from his – skillful? Oh, pock it, let's just call it downright *heroic* actions. Whatever the cause, the sun was shining, the silver was clinking in the till, and right then he felt like the best pockstocking barkeep in all the Freelands.

"And do you know either of the other parties involved?"

"I know the human. Stefan Woodwright. Works as a planner in the Builders Guild building on Artisan Way, but you'd do better to check the barstool on the far right any weekday an hour 'til noon, or half-past sundown." He nodded toward the bar, where he noticed Ardeen flailing about, dark eyes wide, black hair flying from its bun in bristly strands, mouth set in full-lipped snarl as though ready to bite the next hand that flagged her down.

*Should probably get back there to help her soon.*

"The centaur," he continued, "I've never seen before. But from what I hear, he's some well-to-do horse-trader or something."

The staveman nodded as he finished his notes, folded the parchment, and placed it and the stylus in a leather pouch at his hip.

"Master Loradwn," he said, "is the second richest livestock dealer in Angelwood. Tell your proprietor not to hold his breath if he's looking for direct compensation for the damaged window or the table. The Protector's Guild will be lucky to press enough fines off him to pay *our* expenses."

Garret felt an unpleasant twinge in his bowels at the prospect of relaying this news to Master Wallingtok. The nasty little Yllgoni would probably find a way to blame *him* for the whole thing so he could justify docking his pay.

"We'll do what we can to help you out though," the inquisitor continued, running a critical eye over the common room. "You're not too far from our station. I'll bring the boys over a few nights a week. Give you a bit of extra business, eh?"

"Oh, you don't have to do that," said Garret, grinding his teeth to keep his smile from withering into a look of chagrin. The last thing any Freelandish pub wanted was to lose half their clientele by becoming a "stave bar".

"Nonsense! We've been looking for a new watering hole ever since the Busted Barrel went out of business. How're Nemeccaday nights in this place? Pretty lively crowd?"

"They're usually our busiest evenings, yes."

"Well, we'll see you then, then."

The staveman clasped wrists with Garret, then left, his fellows carrying their injured comrades out on stretchers. The barkeep turned back to the bar, a sense of frustration growing inside him. Sometimes running a business in the Freelands could be like building a sandcastle on a beach at high tide.

*Pocking leatherheads,* a cynical voice inside him seethed. *That inquisitor doesn't give a pixie's pimple about giving us "a bit of extra business". Thanks to that byss-blighted centaur, he thinks we're the sort of place that attracts brawlers with money. Now they just want to catch our guests getting drunk and doing bosky shest so they can collect more fines. Talk about bad for business. Kade'll be chucking buckets over this!*

Garret stepped behind the bar just as Ardeen was cramming a final cocktail into a completely full service well. She flashed him one of her rare smiles as he set about clearing unused glasses and appeasing jilted patrons. As a barkeep, Ardeen could be swift and industrious, and her exotic features and hourglass figure certainly gave patrons something to look at while they were being ignored. But as an Yllgoni (and Kade's younger sister no less) she had little patience for the sort of swollen-stalked yawpery that passed for witty banter among the Dragonsbane's regulars.

"Okay," he said, "it's almost time for shift change. Do you want to tend to the guests or stock the bar?"

"Stock!"

She bolted from the bar scarcely glancing at the waves, whistles, and jeers of her patrons.

"All right, fellows! Settle down and gimme your orders and we'll get this place tip-top and trim in no time."

"I'd like to tip-top *her* trim!" some one yelled.

The bar guests roared with laughter, and Garret grabbed his belly and hee-hawed along, as though the joke *weren't* one of the oldest and stupidest he'd ever heard. With practiced precision he cajoled each of his regulars in turn, fixing their usual drinks while trading quips and dolling out sympathy for their troubles in work, family, or romance. In mere minutes the bar was pristine, and adorned with full glasses and happy faces all around. Tossing his bar towel back into a concealed bucket of water and lye, Garret took a moment to survey his handiwork, a look of satisfaction crinkling his eyes and lifting his bristly beard.

*Aye,* he thought. *My bar. This rot-pocked polis might find a million ways to break a man's spirit, but at least I have my bar. My sanctuary. My oasis of humanity in an uncaring desert. My balm for – what the A*byss *is going on over there?*

Just over a patron's slouching shoulder, he noticed a disturbing spectacle. Kade Wallingtok sat at a table by the shattered remains of his window, and there across from him was that kullbung bard. What's more, he was laughing. The stingy, little, sour-faced proprietor was actually laughing!

They stood. They clasped wrists. And that's when Garret realized his worst fears were coming to pass. Fairy Anne (or whatever the bosky snollygoster called himself) had gone over the master barkeep's head and charmed the proprietor into hiring him as an apprentice!

"Ho, Garret!" one of his regulars – a foul-mouthed, slovenly dressed foreman with a big mouth, a bigger belly and an even bigger sense of self-importance – barked out. "Something wrong? You look like my wife when she caught me in the washroom with that Satyress!"

"'Snothing, Mani. Just Wallingtok finding yet another way to shove me face first into the Abyss."

*Pock this place,* the barkeep fumed, smiling at his guests, though it hurt every part of his face. *Pock the Freelands where you can get away with smashing up any place you want if you're rich enough. Pock Angelwood with its transient, muddle-mogged minstrels. And pock Kade Wallingtok for not knowing a good business decision if some one buggered him with it right up his bleeding brown kull!*

That was it! He'd had it! If his idiot boss wanted to put a filthy flimflammer behind his bar, then so be it. Fairy Anne the kullbung bard would soon tire of doing honest work for a living and quit in a matter of weeks. Or maybe he'd stick around long enough to rob the place blind and burn it to the ground. Garret had to admit, there was a significant part of the barkeep that *wanted* him to!

# A Note From the Author

Hail, travellers! I hope you enjoyed your visit to this little corner of Ardyn: the world that lives in my head. If so, you'll be glad to know there are many more stories on the way, each more thrilling than the last.

"But when?" you might ask. "This one was fun, but rather short. I want epics filled with high adventure, characters I know better than my drinking buddies, and exotic locals so vividly described, I can visit them just by closing my eyes!"

Well, my friend, I'd like nothing better than to churn out my tales at break-neck speed, putting into words the countless novels, novellas, novelettes, shorts, and scripts that are constantly roiling about my addled brain. The thing is, for that to happen, I'll need to stop tending bar 40 hours a week and turn crafting fine, fantastic fiction into a full-time career.

"Ho boy," you might groan, "Now comes the part where he hits me up for money!"

No, my dear reader, direct contributions are only one small way you can help. Here are some ways to make a more lasting and less costly contribution to the blessed bounteous bonfire of my art:

- Leave a review on Amazon, Goodreads, or any other site people read. I'd prefer it if you said good things, of course, but any press is good press and any feedback is appreciated.
- Like and follow me on social media. That's @AdamBerkWriter for Twitter, Adam Berk (Writer) on Facebook and my website is adamberkwriter.com

- Lend a book to a friend. Nothing makes you look cooler than being in the know about alternative media. And, friends, I'm as alternative as they come! So don't boggart that literature, man! Pass me around, share me with friends, then get together over beer, liquor, or lattés and laugh about the Freelands' latest insanity.
- Get on my mailing list! Okay, so I'm not the best when it comes to putting out newsletters, so it might be a while before you hear from me, but this is still the second best way to get insider information on upcoming projects, the first being –
- -- send me money! Okay, here it is. If you have a little something extra burning a hole in your pocket, send me a donation through patreon.com/adamberk, and I'll do my best to reward you with inside info and Ardynian easter eggs. Who knows, maybe I'll even write a story about you!

And so, fellow travellers, I thank you most sincerely for your presence and patronage in the world of my dreams. I hope our journey together will be a long one filled with laughs, thrills, and hidden gems of wisdom. And, as I say to all my regulars, drive safe, and come back soon!

Sincerely,
your writer and barkeep,

Adam Berk

# Appendix

## A Guide to Freelandish Slang And Other Terms

**Abis** - Same as Abyss, but pronounced AH-bis. The Freelandish word for hell. Portmanteau word combining the Trophican "Abyss" with the Syndraxan *Ajasi* (pron. AH-ja-see).

**Abyss** – aka the Great Abyss. Place of punishment for evil souls upon their death according to Trophican Ardainite and Evanescicle religions.

**Adder** - also *Addah.* The male organ as great, large or massive. From the Gimadran word Adpha, meaning great, greatness or phallus.

**Brahda** – A term of endearment. Same usage as "brother", although for a friend instead of a literal relative. From the Gimadran *brao dong* meaning family friend.

**Bosky** - Shady, nefarious. From the Old Trophican word for wooded.

**Byss-pit** - A "hell-hole", or an unpleasant place to work, reside, etc. From the words Abyss and pit.

**Byss-blighted** – Same usage as goddamned. rel. byss-blasted, byss-buggered, or byss-pocked.

**Blackrobe** – Term of contempt for an entertainments business professional, referencing the black robes commonly worn by Lascivian Mages. E.g. "I wanted a spectacular battle scene in my play, but the pocking *blackrobes* said we didn't have the budget for it."

**Blatherrach** – Literally, one who assaults others with blather. A person given to voluble, empty talk.

**Bucket** - Common word for chamber pot, i.e. "in the bucket" which is to say, "down the drain".

**Buckethead** – One who, metaphorically speaking, has a chamber pot where his brains should be.

**Bung** - Same usage as "asshole", more commonly in reference to the anatomical part than the type of person (who would more commonly be called a "kullbung").

**Cestodal Grafting Imbuement (CGI)** – Magecraft term for the process of infesting a performer with magically enhanced tine worms to make the subject heal faster and able to attach severed appendages.

**Collywallies** - Feelings of nervous apprehension. From "colic" and the Trophican term, collywobbles.

**Collywald** - A coward. One who is prone to "getting the collywallies".

**Chucking Buckets** - Term for one who is violently enraged. Originated with the famously insane Angelwood Polis Councilman John Hedwig, who after being cheated by a whore in a hotel suite, began throwing chamber pots about the place in a fit of rage.

**Chirk** - to cheer (usually followed by "up"). Also, a shrill, chirping noise.

**Chirkyjerk** - An annoyingly cheerful person.

**Chop** - to banter, usually in an argumentative way, i.e. "just choppin' ya 'bout."

**Clopper** - Racial slur for centaur. More commonly used in the Mystican Countries, especially Medan.

**Cockalorum** - a self-important little man.

**Danglestalk** – Literally a man who is impotent. A man who is dull, boring, and/or lacking sex-drive.

**Dapper** - a waiter, or male servant. Aberration of dapifer.

**Dim Dolly** – Ditz or bimbo. A scatterbrained woman.

**Dolly** - A casual term of endearment, used mostly in the Angelwood entertainment industries. Similar usage to "Babe" or "Sweetie". Variants include, dollywally, dollykins, dollywallykins, etc. From the Gimadran word *doulchika* meaning sweet little girl.

**Dref** - schlock. Corny or overused subject matter as from a song or play. From the

Gimadran word, *drepha* meaning "happy" as used in *pryohka drepha*, a slapstick comedy play. rel. "dreffy"

**Flob** - To stand idly about with no particular purpose. i.e. to "flob about" means to "hang out."

**Frepp** - An awkward, useless person. From the Gimadran *phrepongo*, a criminal who keeps getting caught.

**Freppish** - Similar usage to "wussy", but with more of a furtive, nervous, and possibly guilty connotation.

**Fuzzberries** – Testicles. Also, an actual variety of berry covered with an inedible light purple, fuzzy rind. The taste is like a lychee berry crossed with a kiwifruit.

**Gonnyrot** – The infamous sexually transmitted pox that plagued the early Mystican settlers of the Freelands. The name "Gonny" is a derisive term for Yllgoni people, particularly the sailors from Yllgon who were thought to be the origin of the virus.

**Guvny** – Prudish. From the word governor, the highest state office in the Freelands.

**Hedwig** – i.e. "going hedwig". Angry to the point of insanity. Refers to a famous Angelwood councilman named Hedwig who was known to fly into fits of rage (see chucking buckets).

**Honi** – Vagina; same usage as "pussy". Pronounced HOH-nee. From the Gimadran *Chahoni* or feminine principle. aka Honi-pot or Honi-hive.

**Jawdy** - sleazy. From the Gimadra *Mahkjohdhi* meaning the same.

**Kapistarosolam** – "Land of mindless indulgence". Derisive Syndraxan colloquialism for the Empire of Gimadra

**Koudga** – Unfortunate fellow or chap (usually, but not always, male). From the Gimadran *tikaojana* meaning "a slave who shovels manure".

**Koke** – Same usage as "cool". From the Gimadran *Kahokeh* meaning "rod of authority" - their divine masculine principal.

**Kokachoni** - Copacetic, having pleasant, mellow vibes. From the Gimadran *Kahokeh i'Chahoni* - their divine balance of masculine and feminine energies. *Chahoni* means "cavern of spirits".

**Kull** – Same usage as "ass", usually in reference to the anatomical part, not the type of person.

**Kullbung** – Same usage as "asshole", more commonly in

reference to the type of person, rather than the anatomical part.

**Mog** – Head. Possibly of ancient Medanite origins; same root meaning of the name "Mogu", who is the god of performers, thieves, and basically anyone who has to think on his/her feet.

**Mog-blotted** – muddle-headed, as from regular consumption of alcohol.

**Muddlemog** – a ditzy, careless person. One who obsesses over useless things.

**Palabhandi** – “Backwards land”: the derisive Gimadran colloquialism for the Syndraxan Empire.

**Palacka** – adj. stupid; mentally deficient, or n. one who is lacking in basic mental functions. From the Gimadran *palah gahti* meaning backward-moving.

**Palagong** – slow, apathetic, backwards thinking or moving.

**Pock** – To use sexually. Also used as a generic vulgarity, i.e. “Get that pocking carriage out of the way!” or “The staveman caught me stealing, so now I’m pocked!” Originated with the rampant sexually transmitted diseases when the Freelands were first being colonized.

**Pockstocker** - a whoremonger or pimp.

**Pongo** – A Gimadran term of endearment meaning “big, dumb, and lovable person”. From the Gimadran word *phrepongo* meaning a criminal who always gets caught.

**Poofy** - An effeminate man. Unknown origin.

**Prassy** – Behaving with the fussiness of a spoiled princess. Unknown origin.

**Rach** - Pronounced "rawch". To beat. From the Gimedran *warachee,* which is a type of sandal often used by Gimadran peasant women to beat unruly children.

**Rock-mogged** – Stupid. Having a head like a rock.

**Shest** – Vulgar term for fecal excrement i.e. "trollshest".

**Shest Bucket** – A chamber pot.

**Shestmog** – One with disgusting values. One who has a head full of shest.

**Shest Shover** – Offensive term for a gay man.

**Snarf** – To caress with tongue and mouth.

**Sneck** – A kiss or to kiss.

**Snollygoster** – A clever, unscrupulous person.

**Snollygeck** - To kiss with tongue and groping. To take advantage of sexually.

**Snollyhole** – One's mouth, especially if one is a snollygoster.

**Sparge** – Ejaculate or the act of ejaculating

**Specky** – Amazing to behold. From the Mystican Common word *spectacular.*

**Stalk** – The male member, especially when erect, a.k.a. pockstalk

**Stalkpocker** - Someone (usually a man) who has promiscuous sex with (other) men.

**Stalk-steered** – The condition of being driven primarily by one's desire for sex. syn. wand-willed

**Teedee** – "Very". From the Gimadran, *atido.*

**Twinklies** – Eyes, especially those of a pretty girl (i.e. twinklie blues)

**Vacky** – Shallow. Having no intellectual depth.

**Vix** – A beautiful woman whose beauty endows her with an inflated sense of entitlement. Same usage as "bitch" but with more positive connotation.

# ABOUT THE AUTHOR

In the early 2000s Adam Berk went to college in Los Angeles to study film, and stayed there to try to be a movie star. After growing disgusted with the entertainment industry (and his many unsuccessful attempts to be a part of it), he got a Master's of Professional Writing degree from the University of Southern California and left town. He now lives in Salem Massachusetts where he tends bar, studies the occult with his witchy wife, and writes silly stories about magic and mythic beasts. He has never been happier.

Made in the USA
Middletown, DE
03 September 2023